END GAME

THE REACHER EXPERIMENT BOOK 7

Jude Hardin

1

"My name is Rock Wahlman. In exactly thirty-seven minutes and twenty-nine seconds, I'm going to die."

37:28...

37:27...

37.26...

Wahlman was talking out loud, hoping that the security cameras in the room were still functioning, hoping that the audio would end up on a remote mainframe somewhere, hoping that someone would eventually hear the story he was about to tell.

For reasons that weren't quite clear, the two-star general in charge of an ultra-clandestine intelligence command had decided to destroy the research facility run by the same command—the building that some of the military staffers casually referred to as The Box—where human genetic engineering trials and other medical experiments had been taking place for several years. The doctors and nurses and technicians had been cleared out and the demolition crew had arrived and the stainless steel table Wahlman was tied to had been moved from the medical supply room to a room closer to the center of the basement.

Now, in a matter of minutes, the carefully-placed charges would explode and gravity would bring tons of concrete and glass and wood and metal directly down to where Wahlman was lying. He would be reduced to molecules, and the molecules would be buried in the rubble.

No more Wahlman.

The scumbags who'd rigged the explosives had set a timer for one hour—enough of a window to haul ass and distance themselves from the lung-popping percussive wave sure to be generated by the blast. They'd placed a laptop computer on a wooden chair and had positioned the chair a few feet to the left of Wahlman's table, the digital countdown displayed prominently on an otherwise blank screen, presumably to make Wahlman's final moments on the planet as anxiety-ridden as possible.

"We hope you've enjoyed your stay," one of the sweaty little punks had said, laughing maniacally as he'd exited the room.

Wahlman had not enjoyed his stay. Not even a little bit. He wished that he'd never come back to the facility. He wished that he'd given it more thought. Maybe there could have been another way to accomplish what he'd wanted to accomplish, another way to find out exactly what was going on and gather enough evidence to put a stop to it.

After he'd escaped from the facility the first time, Wahlman had spent a couple of nights in a hotel on the outskirts of Myrtle Beach, and then he'd hitched a ride to

Norfolk and had shown up on the doorstep of an old friend, a guy named Joe Balinger who'd been a fellow Master-At-Arms in the Navy.

"Where's your car?" Joe said. "Did you walk here?"

"I hitchhiked most of the way," Wahlman said.

Joe lived in a nice house in a nice subdivision. Wahlman knew from corresponding with him over the years that he'd started his own security firm after retiring from the Navy, and that he had twenty or so guys working for him now.

Joe was doing okay. More than okay. He was doing great.

He motioned for Wahlman to come on in. Wahlman stepped over the threshold, into the foyer, which was decorated with framed artwork—paintings that looked like they belonged in a museum that specialized in the macabre. The largest of the bunch, a nightmarish scene of a man with a whip and a whistle being torn to shreds by the lion he was supposed to be taming, actually sent a chill down Wahlman's spine, even after all of the real-life horrors he'd experienced recently.

"Kind of takes your breath away, doesn't it?" Joe said.

"Kind of," Wahlman said.

He stared at the painting some more. It was horrible to look at, yet hard to turn away from.

"Chalk one up for the animals," Joe said.

"Where did you get these things?" Wahlman said.

"I got that one in Brazil. You want a beer or something?"

"I was hoping I might be able to stay here for a few days," Wahlman said.

"Okay. You want a beer or something?"

"Sounds good. Mind if I take a quick shower first?"

Wahlman took a shower, and then he joined Joe on the brick patio at the back of the house. A white vinyl privacy fence surrounded the yard, which was probably about a quarter of an acre and needed to be mowed. There was a cooler full of ice and beer out there on the patio and a barbecue grill and some potted plants and a glass-top table with an umbrella and four chairs.

Wahlman pulled a bottle of beer out of the cooler and sat at the table across from Joe.

"Been a while since I've heard from you," Joe said. "What brings you to Norfolk?"

"There has to be a reason?" Wahlman said.

"You know you're welcome any time. But honestly, you don't look so great. How many pounds have you dropped since last time I saw you? Ten? Twenty?"

"More like thirty," Wahlman said.

"So what's going on?"

"Do you really want to know?"

Joe took a long pull from his bottle.

"I don't know," he said. "Do I?"

Wahlman shrugged. "Actually, I'd originally planned to see if you could help me gather some information on a certain colonel in the United States Army," he said. "Some information that I hadn't been able to gather myself."

Joe gazed out at his weedy lawn for a few seconds, and then he reached into the cooler and pulled out two more bottles of beer.

"Maybe you should start from the beginning," he said.

Wahlman told him about the letter that had lured him to New Orleans last October, about witnessing a semi-truck crashing into a canal, about trying to rescue the driver—a man named Darrell Renfro who, as it turned out, looked exactly like Wahlman. He told him about the subsequent events that led to the confirmation that he and Renfro had been cloned from cells taken from a former Army officer named Jack Reacher over a hundred years ago. He told him about the attempts on his life and about the New Orleans homicide detective named Collins and about the warrant for his arrest that was still active and about the online wanted posters and the reward money for capturing him dead or alive. He told him about the private investigator named Feldman, and about the bounty hunter named Decker. He told him about falling in love with Kasey Stielson and about ultimately losing her, and he told him about the elderly hitchhiker named Rusty and about infiltrating the secret research facility off the coast of South Carolina.

"I ended up running into the officer I'd been looking for," Wahlman said. "I forced him to help me escape from the facility."

"Where is he now?" Joe asked.

"I'm pretty sure he's dead," Wahlman said.

"Care to elaborate?"

Wahlman told him about the little joyride he'd taken with Colonel Dorland.

"Not that it's going to make any difference," Wahlman said. "They'll just assign someone else to my case. I need to go back."

5

"To the research facility?"

"I need details. Documentation."

"What do you know so far?"

"Only what Dorland told me. According to him, the Army's current project is being funded by a group of billionaires, investors who are under the impression that the first human clone in the history of the world is going to be produced there at that facility. But that's not the truth. Darrell Renfro and I were the first human clones in the history of the world. We were the first, and that's why we were targeted. That's why our files were erased, and that's why hits were put out on us—because the senior military officers in charge of the current project were afraid that the billionaires would take a hike if they found out about us."

"That's a pretty remarkable story," Joe said. "Seems like the media would be all over it."

"Like stink on shit," Wahlman said. "Except I don't have any proof. Right now it's going to be my word against the military's. Retired Senior Chief Petty Officer Rock Wahlman against the United States Army. Guess who's going to come out on top."

"The Army."

"Correct. And guess whose ass is going to be left flapping in the breeze."

"Yours."

"Exactly. Once I go public, I won't last a day without some kind of protective custody."

"So what's the plan?" Joe said.

"I'm not sure yet," Wahlman said. "I need to find out

exactly what's going on there at the facility. They want to be known for producing the first human clone, but there's more to it than that. Rusty was dying, and he was going there for some kind of treatment. He said that the Army was going to give him a new heart and a new liver and a new pair of lungs. But not with ordinary transplants. Something different. Something new. He wouldn't go into it, but I'm wondering if the Army is planning to produce clones for the purpose of harvesting their organs."

"I doubt it," Joe said. "Ethical concerns aside, I just don't see how it would work. If you need a new heart, you need it now. Not ten years from now. Or twenty. Or however long it would take."

"Yeah. So I don't know."

Joe pulled two more beers out of the cooler.

"Is there anything I can do to help?" he said.

"Maybe," Wahlman said. "Do you still have that admiral's uniform you confiscated in Okinawa that time?"

2

Joe still had the uniform. It was in a closet in one of his spare bedrooms, covered in plastic. If Wahlman had been at his normal weight, he never would have been able to get into it.

But Wahlman was not at his normal weight. He'd lost thirty pounds.

The admiral that the uniform had belonged to was a tall and lanky Academy man named Swanson. He'd developed a serious gambling problem while stationed overseas, and he'd started taking kickbacks from a company that exported canned tuna from Japan to the United States. In exchange for a certain number of dollars, the admiral allowed the company to load a certain number of crates onto a certain number of military transport planes headed for San Francisco. The company saved a bundle on shipping charges, and the admiral collected a tidy sum to help feed his blackjack habit. Everybody happy, until a surprise inspection revealed that a number of the crates contained handguns instead of tuna. A major investigation followed, and one of the company executives flipped, and Admiral

Swanson was arrested and flown to San Diego to be court martialed. Two Master-At-Arms petty officers—Rock Wahlman and Joe Balinger—had been assigned to sort and catalog the admiral's personal belongings and move them from the house he'd been renting in town to a storage unit on the base, where in all likelihood they would remain for decades. Knowing that—and knowing that the admiral probably wouldn't be an admiral much longer anyway—Joe had tossed one of the dress uniforms onto the discard pile and had kept it for a souvenir.

A souvenir that just happened to fit a somewhat-emaciated Rock Wahlman perfectly.

"Looks good on you," Joe said. "You're not really thinking about—"

"Why not?" Wahlman said. "It's not like I have a lot to lose at this point."

"I just don't see how you could get away with it."

"Got any better ideas?"

"Yeah. Let's go drink some more beer."

Joe exited the room. Wahlman took the uniform off, draped the plastic over it and hung it in the closet. He slipped back into his grungy road clothes, knowing that Joe would have offered him something clean to wear if they had been anywhere near the same size. Joe was about a foot shorter than Wahlman, and he'd always been fond of things like beer and fried chicken and apple cobbler. He'd been a frequent member of what some of the sailors joking called the Fat Boy Club—the early-morning workout sessions you had to attend if you flunked a routine physical fitness test—

and he was probably a little chubbier now than he'd been back then.

On his way out of the bedroom, Wahlman noticed a picture of a woman on Joe's dresser. She was very beautiful. Dark hair, eyes as warm as cinnamon toast. He picked up the photograph and looked at it, and then he walked back out to the patio.

There was a fresh beer waiting for him on the table. He took a sip, slid into the same chair he'd been sitting in earlier.

"I could go out there on Saturday," he said.

"Out where?" Joe said.

"To the research facility. You know how it is at places like that on the weekends. Quiet. Laidback. Duty staff only, everyone wishing they were out fishing or playing tennis or doing whatever it is they like to do."

"Duty staff or not, they're not going to let you just waltz on in and take over," Joe said. "I don't care what kind of uniform you're wearing."

"We'll need to draft a fake set of orders," Wahlman said.

"We?"

"And of course I'll need a driver."

Joe picked at the label on his beer bottle.

"I don't think I can afford to get involved," he said. "I recently got engaged to be married, and—"

"I saw her picture on the dresser," Wahlman said. "She's very pretty."

"She's also very pregnant. We were planning on getting married anyway, but the baby puts a whole new spin on things."

"Congratulations," Wahlman said.

"Thanks."

"Is it still okay if I stay here for a few days?"

Joe didn't say anything. He picked at his label and chewed on his lower lip. He'd obviously given it some thought, and he'd obviously decided to withdraw his offer to help Wahlman with his problems. Which was understandable. Wahlman's problems were big problems. Life and death problems. Joe had always been a good friend, but every good friend has his or her limits. Apparently the notion of aiding and abetting a fugitive from justice in his quest to infiltrate a secret government research facility by impersonating a senior Naval officer had set off some sort of alarm in Joe's soon-to-be-a-family man consciousness.

And that was okay. Wahlman had become accustomed to doing everything alone. He would get through this, somehow.

Those had been his thoughts as he drained the last few ounces of beer from a sweaty green bottle out there on Joe's patio.

But now, as he watched the seconds tick off the timer, he wasn't so sure.

3

Joe had given Wahlman the admiral's uniform, along with a set of summer whites with E-6 patches sewn onto the sleeves, and he'd loaned him some money, enough to rent a car and a hotel room for a few days.

Wahlman had chosen a generic-looking four-door sedan, a black one that closely resembled some of the official government vehicles he'd seen at the research facility, and he'd driven it back down to the Myrtle Beach area and had checked into the same place he'd stayed at previously. He used one of the desktop computers in the lobby to create a fake set of orders for the fake flag officer he was planning to become, knowing that the paperwork wouldn't pass any sort of rigorous inspection process and pretty much betting his life that it wouldn't have to. He bought some dark brown hair dye at a nearby pharmacy and a dark brown mustache at a nearby costume shop, and he bought an audio recording device about the size of a quarter at a nearby electronics store.

Now all he needed was a driver.

It was a crucial part of the plan, because generals and admirals never drove themselves anywhere. They always had a personal assistant assigned to them, an E-4 or an E-5 or an E-6 who served as a chauffeur and a secretary and a baggage handler and an errand runner. Skate duty, as long as the officer you were assigned to wasn't an asshole.

Wahlman got up early Saturday morning and drove to an employment agency that specialized in daily work for daily pay. The place wasn't scheduled to open for another hour, but there were already a hundred or so men and women standing in line. Wahlman parked his car and climbed out and walked forward from the back of the queue, searching for male candidates between the ages of twenty-five and thirty-five who could fit into Joe Balinger's old petty officer first class uniform and who weren't exhibiting any major withdrawal symptoms from whatever substance they were trying to earn enough money to purchase after work.

A tweaker who could have posed for one of the ghastly paintings in Joe's foyer shouted for Wahlman to get his ass to the back of the line.

"I'm not here to work," Wahlman said. "I'm here to hire."

"What kind of job?" the tweaker said.

"The kind you're not qualified for."

Wahlman kept walking. A few seconds later, he felt a tap on his right shoulder.

It was the tweaker.

"How do you know what I'm not qualified for?" the guy said.

His breath smelled horrible. Like a rat that had drowned in a urinal. A week ago.

"Get lost," Wahlman said.

"Give me five bucks and I'll leave you alone."

"I'm not giving you shit."

"Then I'm not leaving you alone."

Wahlman kept walking. The tweaker followed.

"You should get back in line," Wahlman said.

"I already lost my place now," the tweaker said.

"Not my problem."

"It's going to be your problem when I slap you upside your head."

Wahlman laughed. He reached into his pocket and pulled out a five dollar bill.

"Here you go," he said. "Take the day off."

The tweaker grabbed the money and scurried away like a squirrel with a peanut.

A guy with a three-day beard and a belly the size of a watermelon stepped over and took his place.

"I heard you're hiring," the guy said.

Wahlman looked him over. He was the right size, but that was about all he had going for him. Long stringy hair, flip-flops, crimson roadmaps for eyes.

"You got a driver's license?" Wahlman said.

"Yes."

"I'm only going to need you for one day."

"That's fine."

"Hundred bucks."

"That's fine."

"It's going to be a long day."

The guy clawed at the stubble on his chin.

"Most of the outfits that hire through the agency do half days on Saturdays," he said.

"If that's what you're looking for, then you need to keep looking," Wahlman said.

"How long you plan on working?"

"As long as it takes."

The guy shrugged.

"Okay," he said.

"I'll need you to get a haircut," Wahlman said. "And a shave."

"I don't have any money," the guy said.

"I'll take it out of your pay," Wahlman said.

The guy shrugged again. Said okay again.

Wahlman checked the guy's driver's license. His name was Donald Puhler. The address on the license was a rooming house not far from the employment agency. Puhler admitted that he didn't live there anymore. He said that he didn't live anywhere anymore.

Wahlman took him to a barbershop, waited in the parking lot until the place was supposed to open for business, and then waited twenty more minutes until the place actually did open for business. There were two barber's chairs, but there was only one barber on duty, a guy in his late twenties or early thirties who'd spent a great amount of time in gymnasiums and tattoo parlors. His nametag said Nate. He smiled and told Wahlman and Puhler good morning and said that he would be right with them.

"Just need to get everything set up real quick," he said.

Wahlman nodded, leaned against the doorjamb and folded his arms across his chest.

Puhler walked over to one the wooden benches against the wall and grabbed a magazine. He thumbed through the slick pages for a couple of minutes, and then he stood and gazed through the barbershop's plate glass window. There was a bakery across the street and a television repair shop and a furniture store. Wahlman figured Puhler was looking at the bakery.

"We'll get some breakfast when we leave here," Wahlman said.

"Sounds good," Puhler said.

Nate opened the safe behind the counter, pulled out a cash drawer and slid it into the computerized register. He pushed some buttons and the drawer popped back open and he counted the money and pushed some more buttons and ran a report tape and jammed the drawer back into its slot. The entire process took about ten minutes.

In a perfect world, the guy responsible for opening a place up for the day would arrive thirty minutes prior to the posted opening time and would promptly take care of everything that needed to be taken care of. It was the way Wahlman would have handled it if he had been a barber. Or a baker. Or a TV repairman. It was the Navy way. It was Wahlman's way. No other way made sense. Maybe there weren't usually any customers in the shop that early. Maybe that was the reason Nate had become such a lazy shitbird slacker. Or maybe it was just the opposite. Maybe Nate had been a lazy shitbird slacker all along and there weren't any customers in the shop that early because everyone knew what a lazy shitbird slacker he was. He finally finished with the register and grabbed a white cape with little blue sailboats on it from an overhead cabinet and stepped over to the barber's chair closest to the entrance.

"All set," he said.

Puhler climbed into the chair. Nate draped the cape around him, tilted him back to the sink and gave him a quick shampoo and rinse. He patted him dry with a towel and asked him what kind of cut he wanted.

"It needs to be short enough to pass a military inspection," Wahlman said. "And give him a shave, too."

"I don't do that," Nate said.

"You don't do what?" Wahlman said.

"Shaves."

Wahlman glanced up at the painted wooden sign mounted to the wall behind the register. The sign listed the services provided by the shop, the different types of haircuts and beard trims you could get, along with the prices the shop charged for each service.

The word *SHAVE* was at the bottom of the list.

Wahlman pointed toward the sign.

"It says right there that you—"

"Some of the guys who work here do shaves," Nate said. "I'm not one of them."

"What time will the guys who'll do what the sign says they'll do be here?" Wahlman said.

"About an hour from now. You want to wait?"

"No. You can either give the man in your chair a shave, or we're going to walk out of here and never come back."

"Are you his dad or something?" Nate said. "Why can't he—"

"I'm his boss," Wahlman said. "And right now I'm your boss too. Give him a shave."

Nate laughed. He tapped Puhler on the shoulder.

"What kind of haircut do you want?" he said.

Wahlman walked over and grabbed the cape and pulled it off of Puhler.

"Let's go," Wahlman said.

Puhler climbed out of the chair.

"You still owe me for a haircut," Nate said.

"How do you figure that?" Wahlman said.

"I already shampooed him. I could have been halfway through with the cut by now if you hadn't started—"

"Let's go," Wahlman said again.

He turned and headed toward the door. Puhler followed.

Nate stepped over and grabbed Puhler by the arm.

"Somebody needs to pay me," Nate said.

Wahlman wrapped his hand around Nate's wrist.

Twisted it counterclockwise.

Heard it snap.

Nate screamed. It was a high-pitched wail, incongruent with the manly physique and body art. He started stomping around the shop, whimpering, cupping the wounded joint with the hand that still functioned, the expression on his face a combination of disbelief and agony.

There was a phone by the register. Nate staggered over

there and reached for the receiver, but Wahlman beat him to it.

"I don't have time for this shit," Wahlman said.

He clocked Nate with the cordless handset, just above the right ear. Nate collapsed to the floor, banging his chin on the counter on the way down.

Puhler was still standing by the door.

"Now what?" he said.

"Get back in the chair," Wahlman said. "I'll cut your hair myself."

4

Wahlman gave Puhler a crewcut with a set of clippers, and he gave him a shave with a straight razor. He only cut him twice. Used an alum block from one of the drawers behind the chair to help stop the bleeding.

A customer walked into the shop, turned around and walked back out.

Probably unimpressed with Wahlman's skills.

Nate was still unconscious behind the counter when Wahlman and Puhler left the shop.

It was almost ten by the time they made it to the hotel.

"Take a shower, and then put those on," Wahlman said, pointing toward the set of summer whites on the bed.

"You want me to dress up like a Navy guy?" Puhler said.

"Right."

"Isn't that illegal?"

"Yes."

Puhler clawed at his chin. It was smooth now. No more stubble. One of the little cuts started bleeding again.

"I don't want to do anything that might get me in

trouble," Puhler said. "Not for a hundred bucks."

"How about two hundred?" Wahlman said.

"How about two-fifty?"

"Okay."

Puhler walked to the bathroom and closed the door. A few seconds later, the shower started running.

Wahlman stripped naked and secured the little disc-shaped audio recorder between his butt cheeks with a piece of tape, and then he put the admiral's uniform on. Once the recorder was switched on, it would only run for about an hour before the battery went dead, so Wahlman left it off for now. It would be there when he needed it.

Puhler was in the shower for a long time. He actually started singing at one point. Wahlman recognized the tune. It was an old country and western line dance song. Puhler was really belting it out. Wahlman hoped he was better at driving than he was at singing.

Wahlman had been thinking about Kasey Stielson. He'd been thinking about her a lot. He'd never stopped loving her. He had no idea where she was now, but he still had the password to their old *Message Moi* account. *Message Moi* was a free voicemail service for people who didn't have phones or who didn't want to give out their numbers for one reason or another. The password to the account was in Wahlman's wallet. He'd written it down on a strip of paper. He wanted to tell Kasey how he felt about everything before leaving for the research facility, knowing that it might be his last chance. Knowing that he might not make it out of the facility alive this time.

He sat on the bed by the nightstand and punched the toll-free number into the room phone and entered the password and spent the next few minutes pouring his heart out.

Of course it was possible that Kasey would never receive the message. It was possible that she would never log into the *Message Moi* account again for as long as she lived. Wahlman hoped that she would, but there was nothing he could do to make it happen.

Puhler finally came out of the shower and put the E-6 uniform on.

"The shoes don't fit," he said. "They're way too small."

"Wear your flip-flops," Wahlman said. "Nobody's going to see your feet anyway."

"What exactly is it that we're going to be doing?"

"All you have to do is drive. I'll be getting out of the car for a while, and you'll be waiting for me in a parking lot."

"That's it?"

"Basically. If I think of anything else, I'll tell you on the way."

They took the ferry over to the island, stayed in the car the whole time. Wahlman didn't want to walk around on the observation deck where people could see him. The uniform he was wearing was a major head turner. Uniforms tended to attract attention anyway, but an admiral's uniform tended to attract it exponentially. The gold stars, the power they represented. It was something most people just didn't see every day. Puhler stayed in the driver seat, alone in front like a chauffeur, and Wahlman stayed directly behind him, shielded from casual view by Puhler himself and by the car's tinted windows.

When they disembarked from the ferry, Wahlman gave Puhler directions to Highway 30, and then he showed him the discreet turnoff that led to the research facility.

Puhler pulled to the side of the highway and braked to a stop before steering into the tunnel of dense foliage.

"You think they'll just wave us on in?" he said.

Wahlman handed him the fake set of orders he'd printed.

"Give these to the guy at the gate," he said. "Most sentries aren't going to give an admiral a hard time. Most sentries are going to be nervous, fearful that their lives will be ruined if they don't salute crisply enough and say *sir* enthusiastically enough."

"What if this particular sentry starts asking a bunch of questions?" Puhler said.

"I'll climb out of the car and make him wish he hadn't," Wahlman said.

Puhler nodded. He slid the shifter into gear and headed into the tunnel.

5

Kasey Stielson slid the glass door open and walked outside. She sat in one of the cushioned deck chairs and stared out at the vast Virginia wilderness that had become her back yard. The family would be safe here, her father had told her. Only a handful of people knew about this place, he'd said. Totally off the grid.

So far, so good. Nobody had shown up looking for Rock Wahlman. No private investigators or bounty hunters or professional assassins. This had been a safe place, just as her father had said it would be, and Kasey wanted to make sure it continued to be a safe place. For her, and for her parents, and especially for her fifteen-year-old daughter, Natalie, who'd originally considered the situation a grand adventure, but whose attitude toward it had been steadily deteriorating over the past few weeks.

Understandable for a girl that age, but still a bit trying at times.

The conversations had become somewhat typical.

"When can we go home?" Natalie had said, yesterday afternoon.

"I don't know," Kasey had said.

"I miss my friends."

"I know you do."

"It's not fair."

"You're right. It's not."

"Can't I at least have my phone back?"

"Maybe in a few days."

"You always say that!"

And so on and so forth. Round and round, on a daily basis.

There was one functional cell phone in the house, to be used for emergencies only. Kasey had been following that particular rule for the most part, although lately she'd been checking the *Message Moi* account she and Rock had set up, knowing that she shouldn't be using the phone on a regular basis but doing it anyway.

Doing it once a day, every day, out there on the deck where she was sitting now.

Because while Natalie was the most important person in her life, and while nothing would ever change that, she had to admit that she missed Rock.

Severely.

She'd been thinking about him lately.

She'd been thinking about him a lot.

And the reasons weren't altogether personal. If he had somehow managed to resolve his problems with the Army, it was something she needed to know about. And if the New Orleans Police Department had caught up to him and had taken him into custody, she needed to know about that too.

She needed to know what was going on so that she and Natalie and Dean and Betsy really could go home and resume some sort of normal existence.

Kasey's parents had occasionally mentioned the possibility that Rock had been killed, but Kasey refused to give that sort of talk any credence. She somehow knew that he was still alive, still out there somewhere.

She picked up the phone and punched in the number and entered the password and waited for the robotic attendant to tell her what it always told her, that she didn't have any new messages.

Only this time it didn't tell her that.

This time, it told her that she did have a new message.

Her heart skipped a beat, and a few seconds later she heard the voice she'd been longing to hear.

6

The guard at the gate stepped up to the car and motioned for Puhler to roll the window down.

"Show him the papers," Wahlman said. "Try to look confident. Try to say as little as possible."

Puhler rolled down the window.

"This is a restricted area," the guard said. "Authorized personnel only."

Puhler didn't say anything. He handed the guy the orders. The guy glanced down at the first page, and then he leaned in and glanced into the back seat. His eyes got big and he popped to attention and saluted, as if some sort of switch had been thrown.

Wahlman returned the salute from inside the car.

The guard opened the gate, and Puhler drove through and steered around to the back of the building.

"Told you he'd be nervous," Wahlman said.

"I'm nervous too," Puhler said.

"There's a portal to the PTS inside that shack over there," Wahlman said. "I'm going to get out of the car and use it to get inside the building. I might be a while."

"PTS?"

"Pneumatic transport system."

"How long will you be gone?"

"I don't know."

"What if they find out you're not really an admiral?"

"They'll take me into custody."

"Right. And I'm just supposed to sit here and—"

"They won't find out," Wahlman said.

Puhler dabbed at the sweat on his forehead with a paper napkin he'd saved from breakfast.

"If they take you into custody, they'll probably take me into custody too," he said.

"Probably," Wahlman said.

"I don't remember that being part of the deal."

"Give me two hours," Wahlman said. "If I'm not back by then—"

"What about my pay?"

"It's in a drawer, back at the hotel. There's a room key in the glove compartment."

"So what's stopping me from hauling ass as soon as you get out of the car?"

"You don't want to do that," Wahlman said.

"Why not?" Puhler said.

"Because, if you do, it means that you're betting against me making it in and out of the facility in a smooth and timely manner. Which, of course, is what I intend to do. If I come out here within the next two hours and see that you've left me stranded, I will hunt you down and rip your throat out with my bare hands."

Puhler dabbed at the sweat on his forehead some more.

"All right," he said. "Two hours."

Wahlman figured that if he wasn't back in two hours that he would probably be dead. But there was no point in letting Puhler in on that particular tidbit. No point in making him more nervous than he already was.

Wahlman climbed out of the car and walked over to the shack. There was a United States Navy Master-At-Arms sitting at the desk, drinking coffee and reading a paperback novel. He nearly fell out of his chair when Wahlman opened the door and stepped over the threshold.

"Attention on deck!" the guard shouted.

It was an automatic reaction, drilled into him since his first day at boot camp. Kind of ridiculous under the circumstances, considering he was the only person attending the shack.

He stood erect and looked straight ahead. Thumbs lined up along the seams of his pants, shoes at a forty-five degree angle.

"At ease," Wahlman said.

The guard relaxed his stance. He was probably around twenty-five years old. Blond hair, blue eyes, freckles on his cheeks. His uniform was slightly faded, but the patches on his sleeves looked brand new. Which told Wahlman that he'd just recently gotten his crow—his promotion from seaman to petty officer third class. His nametag said Hurkley.

"How may I assist you, sir?" he said.

"The general's meeting me here later," Wahlman said. "In the meantime, he wants me to familiarize myself with the facility and get a breakdown on the research that's being conducted."

"General Foss is coming here? Today?"

"It's a surprise inspection," Wahlman said. "So don't tell anyone."

"I won't, sir."

"Do you know how to operate the PTS?"

"Yes, sir. But—"

"Take me inside. Then I'll need someone with the right kind of clearance to show me around and explain the procedures that are being performed here."

"Dr. Walker is here today," Hurkley said. "She would be the person for you to talk to."

"Great. Take me to her."

"I'm not supposed to leave my post, sir. We're a little short-staffed today, so I'll need to call the security office and—"

"Just get me inside and show me the way to Dr. Walker's office," Wahlman said. "It'll only take a few minutes."

Hurkley raked his hair back with his fingers. Tensely. Nervously. There was a senior military officer standing three feet in front of him, ordering him to abandon his post. Ordering him to do something he'd been taught never to do, no matter what. It was a true dilemma, and Wahlman knew that it could go either way. Hurkley could either disregard military protocol and potentially face severe consequences somewhere down the line, or he could disobey a direct order and assuredly face severe consequences right now.

He stood there thinking it over.

Wahlman figured he would obey the order. He was counting on it. Because once you really thought it through, obeying the order was the only logical course of action. It was the only way to maybe not get in trouble at all. It wasn't likely that any sort of security issue would come up while Hurkley was gone. It wasn't likely that anyone would ever know. Especially on a Saturday.

"Sir, I'll be happy to escort you to the portal closest to Dr. Walker's office," Hurkley said. "Should I call and let her know that you're on your way."

"That won't be necessary," Wahlman said. "We want it to be a surprise. Remember?"

"Yes, sir. A surprise."

"And I'll need for you to come and get me when I'm finished."

"Yes, sir. I'll write down the number to the phone here in the shack, and you can call me as soon as you're ready to exit the facility."

Hurkley tore a strip of paper from a notepad he'd been doodling on, wrote down the number and handed it to Wahlman. He helped Wahlman into the transport capsule, and a few seconds later they were on their way.

7

The door to Dr. Walker's office was open. She was sitting at a desk, staring at a computer screen. She wore a white lab coat with her name embroidered over the pocket and a white blouse with tiny blue and red polka dots on it and a wristwatch with a black leather band. Dark brown hair, shoulder length, with a few strands of gray on top, just enough to let people know that she was forty-something and proud of it. Maybe she would start having it dyed in a few years. Maybe not. She certainly didn't need to. She was very attractive, and she was going to remain attractive, in Wahlman's opinion, no matter what happened with her hair.

She wasn't wearing a uniform under the lab coat, which meant that she was probably a civilian. Which meant that she wasn't going to be nearly as intimidated by the stars on Wahlman's sleeves as Hurkley and the guard at the gate had been.

Wahlman slid his hand into the back of his pants and switched on the audio recorder. Dr. Walker glanced up from her monitor screen as he stepped into the office.

"May I help you?" she said.

"Hello," Wahlman said. "I'm Admiral Callahan. Naval Intelligence. I know you weren't expecting me, but—"

"Please, come in. Have a seat."

Wahlman stepped forward, sat in the steel and vinyl chair at the side of the desk. He told Dr. Walker the same set of lies that he'd told Hurkley.

"I thought you might be able to show me around before General Foss gets here," he said.

"I'm just curious as to why he chose to do this on a Saturday."

"I'm sure he has his reasons."

"Right. Well, I was just finishing up with some research statistics, and I was planning on going home after that. My granddaughter has a soccer game this afternoon, and—"

"Granddaughter?" Wahlman said. "You're kidding. You don't look nearly old enough."

"Thank you. I have two already, a boy and a girl. Would you like to see some pictures?"

"I would love to," Wahlman said.

He scooted closer to where Dr. Walker was sitting, and she showed him some photographs on the computer. Wahlman went on about what lovely children they were, and how much the little girl looked like her grandmother.

"I suppose I could miss her game this one time," Dr. Walker said.

"All I need is a quick tour," Wahlman said. "Maybe you can show me around and still make it out to watch her play."

Dr. Walker nodded. She closed out the work she'd been

doing on her computer, and then she led Wahlman out of the office and down the hall to an elevator. She pressed a button with a picture of an arrow pointing upward on it, and the stainless steel door slid open immediately. Wahlman followed her into the compartment. It was big enough for the two of them, but just barely. Their arms touched when they turned around and faced the door.

"How much do you already know about the work we're doing here?" Dr. Walker asked, pressing the button for the fourth floor.

"I know you're conducting experiments that involve genetic engineering," Wahlman said. "I know you're attempting to produce the world's first human clone."

"That's really just the tip of the iceberg," Dr. Walker said. "In fact, we already have several mature clones. That was the easy part."

The elevator reached its destination. The door opened, and Wahlman followed Dr. Walker out into the hallway. She led him through a confusing maze of corridors, and finally to a solid steel door guarded by a keypad and a fingerprint scanner.

"Where are we?" Wahlman said.

"This is the main laboratory. You're going to see some things in here that very few people have ever seen. If you're the least bit squeamish—"

"I'm not," Wahlman said.

"Have you ever witnessed a surgical procedure or an autopsy?"

"Yes."

"Okay. You should be fine."

She punched some numbers into the keypad, and then she pressed her right index finger against the scanner. The door opened automatically. Inside, there was an anteroom with a desk and a computer and some cabinets and a couch. Dr. Walker used a key to unlock the wooden door at the far end of the room.

Wahlman followed her into the lab.

She switched on some lights.

The room was enormous. You could have played basketball in there. It reminded Wahlman of his high school biology lab, only ten times bigger. There were tables and stools and sinks and gas outlets. Beakers and burners and tubes and clamps. Microscopes, equipment bins, portable lights that looked like they belonged on a construction site.

A huge glass tank with partitions positioned vertically every three or four feet had been built into the wall on the left side of the room. Like an aquarium, only there weren't any fish swimming around in it. Instead, each section housed what appeared to be a well-preserved human cadaver. Adult males in their early twenties, suspended in a substance that resembled lime-flavored gelatin.

"Looks more like something you might expect to see at a medical school," Wahlman said, gesturing toward the tank.

"What do you mean?" Dr. Walker said.

"The bodies. You're planning to dissect them, right?"

"Why would we do that?"

"I just assumed that a tank full of dead people would be for—"

"They're not cadavers," Dr. Walker said. "Those are the clones. And they're very much alive."

8

Kasey had listened to the message dozens of times. She'd gone inside for a notebook and had transcribed it word for word. Rock had told her how much he loved her, and how much he missed her, and how sorry he was that it hadn't worked out. He'd told her how close he was to finding the answers he needed to find. He'd been to a secret military research facility on an island off the coast of South Carolina, and he was going back there today in an effort to obtain more details. More evidence. Enough to take to the media. Enough to break the story on the world stage. If he was successful, his problems could potentially be resolved in a matter of days. If he was not successful, it wasn't likely that he would make it off the island alive.

Which was why he'd wanted Kasey to know the alias he'd been using and the name of the hotel he'd been staying at. So that if he died, she could make an anonymous phone call and point the authorities in the right direction.

Of course all of that had depended on Kasey retrieving the voicemail in the first place. Which, Rock admitted, was a long shot. He could only hope that she would, and that the facts pertaining to his predicament would eventually be told.

Kasey called the hotel, hoping that he hadn't left the room yet, or that he'd gone and returned already, but there was no answer.

The back door swung open and Natalie stepped out onto the deck.

"Hi, Mom," she said.

"Hi."

"What are you doing?"

Kasey closed the notebook.

"Nothing," she said.

"I saw you using the phone."

"Maybe you just imagined it."

"It's not fair, Mom. Why do you get to use the phone and I don't?"

"Because I'm a grownup and you're a kid?"

"I'm fifteen."

"Like I said."

Natalie pulled a chair over and sat next to Kasey.

"Please, Mom. Just one phone call."

"You want the bad guys to find us?"

"I want my life back."

Natalie climbed out of the chair and started to walk away.

"Wait," Kasey said. "There's something I need to talk to you about. Serious business. Come here and sit back down."

"Are you going to let me use the phone?"

"No."

"Then I'm not going to sit back down."

"Fine. Stay where you are. Just listen to me for a minute, okay?"

Natalie folded her arms across her chest and leaned against the back door.

"I'm listening," she said.

"I've been using the phone to check for messages on a voicemail service," Kasey said.

"Messages from who?"

"Rock."

"I thought you were done with him."

"I still love him," Kasey said.

Natalie returned to the chair.

"He's been leaving messages for you?" she said.

"He left one today. This is the first time I've heard from him since I broke it off. It sounds like he's really close to getting to the bottom of all this."

"That's good, right?"

"Yes. But he's going somewhere today that might be very dangerous."

"He's done dangerous things before," Natalie said. "He can take care of himself."

"I know. And I know there's no point in worrying. But I can't help it. I feel like I should be there for him. I feel like he needs me right now."

"Then go."

"But you need me too."

"I'll be fine, Mom. It's not like I'm alone here. And it's not like I'm a little kid, either. Even though you seem to think I am."

"I'm still not sure if I'm going to go or not," Kasey said. "I'm going to have to think about it some more. And of course I'll need to talk it over with Mom and Dad."

"If you love him, you should go."

"Do you really think so?"

"Yes. But you should leave the phone here."

"Ah. An ulterior motive. Now I see how it is."

"I'm just joking, Mom."

Kasey smiled.

"I know you are, sweetheart," she said. "I know you are."

9

Wahlman stood there and stared into the glass tank.

"What do you mean they're alive?" he said.

"They're being kept in a hypometabolic state," Dr. Walker said. "We provide their nutrition and oxygenation parenterally."

"Why?"

"So they'll be ready for us when we need them."

"Need them for what?"

Dr. Walker stepped closer to the tank. She reached out and touched the glass with her fingertips.

"We were supposed to perform the first transplant last week," she said. "But the donor never showed up. We're still not sure what happened to him."

"So you're harvesting organs?" Wahlman said. "That's what this is all about?"

"No. Not at all. Are you familiar with the part of the brain called the right temporal lobe?"

"I'm not a scientist," Wahlman said. "My background is in law enforcement."

"The right temporal lobe is the center of self-awareness and autobiographical memory," Dr. Walker said. "It's basically the core essence of a person. It's what you are, what you've become over the course of your lifetime. All of your thoughts and experiences, wrapped up in a section of tissue that would fit in the palm of your hand. What we're hoping to accomplish is to transplant that center of self-awareness and autobiographical memory from one person to another—from the donor to the donor's genetic duplicate—thereby extending the lifespan of that particular individual by as much as a hundred percent."

"So you're basically going to be doing brain transplants," Wahlman said.

"You could think of it like that if you want to. But it's not really the entire brain. Just a little part of it."

"So you could take an old sick person and transfer his or her consciousness into a young healthy person?"

"Yes. In fact, the donor who was supposed to show up last week was very ill. His name was Rusty. We're thinking he must have died while he was traveling to get here, although we don't know that for sure yet. This is his clone over here."

Dr. Walker stepped to the right and pointed toward one of the creepy human figures suspended in green gelatin.

"That guy has to be at least twenty years old," Wahlman said, pointing toward Rusty's clone. "So you've been working on this for decades?"

"Believe it or not, the man you're looking at now was produced from a single cell six months ago," Dr. Walker said.

"How is that possible?"

"The accelerated growth medium. The AGM. It allows us to produce a full-grown specimen in months instead of years."

"The green stuff?" Wahlman said.

"Yes. Quite revolutionary. It's really the only reason any of this is possible. The technology to produce human clones has been around for a long time, and the theory behind temporal lobe transplantation has been around for a long time, but the AGM is what has allowed us to combine the two in a practical way."

"So when I get old, you could transfer all of my thoughts and memories into a younger version of myself?" Wahlman said.

"That's it in a nutshell," Dr. Walker said.

"Let's say it works," Wahlman said. "Let's say you do all that and I'm good to go for another fifty years or whatever. What's going to stop me from doing it again and again?"

"You can't do it again and again," Dr. Walker said. "You can only do it once."

"Why?"

"Because of the AGM. I don't want to bore you with a bunch of technical details, so let me just say that it does funny things to the immune system. Immediately after being removed from the tank, the clones become severely allergic to that particular chain of molecules. Once the transplant is completed, the clones can never go anywhere near the AGM again. If they do, they die. It's sort of a built-in safeguard against abusing the technology. Although, to be honest, it was entirely unintentional."

"What about some of the other ethical implications?" Wahlman said. "You're growing genetic duplicates in a laboratory. These are living, breathing human beings, right? You grew a young Rusty, and you were essentially planning to murder him so that the old Rusty could live longer. Murder is murder, right? How can anyone with a conscience agree to be part of that?"

"The AGM causes the right temporal lobe to shut down very early in the cloning process," Dr. Walker said. "The clones are basically brain dead until we perform the transplant. So taking them out of the tank and using them for our purposes is not like murder at all. More like pulling the plug on a comatose patient when there's absolutely no hope for recovery."

Wahlman didn't like that answer. What the Army was doing was wrong, in his opinion.

Very wrong.

"I'm assuming you're planning on taking the whole thing mainstream at some point," he said. "So you can make a bunch of money off of it."

"The investors should do well," Dr. Walker said. "We're still in the trial phases, of course, but if the procedure works, it'll be like getting a second chance at life. Who wouldn't sign up for that?"

It was an interesting question. If you could suddenly inhabit a younger and physically-stronger version of yourself while retaining all of your current knowledge and memories, would you do it? Would you really want to live through your twenties again? Your thirties? And so on.

Wahlman figured that most people would say yes. But he wondered if most people would learn anything from all of the mistakes they'd made along the way. He wondered if they would muff things up just as much the second time around.

"So when are you planning to put all of these theories to the test?" he said.

"Another donor is scheduled to arrive a week from Monday," Dr. Walker said. "His clone is the one on the very end over there. We've provided an escort for the donor this time, so there shouldn't be any issues getting him here. We're planning to perform the surgery a week from Tuesday."

Wahlman figured he had enough to take to the media now. There would be no surgery a week from Tuesday. Or ever. Or at least for a long time. Because by Monday it would be revealed that the first human clones in the history of the world were not produced at this facility, but instead were produced over forty years ago. They were given identities and bogus family histories and placed in orphanages and recently targeted for elimination to conceal the fact that they ever existed in the first place. The funding for the current project would dry up immediately. The case would be in the courts for years. Decades maybe. General Foss, and everyone else who'd been involved in the cover-up, would be arrested, and there wasn't a judge on the planet who would grant any of them any sort of bail in a case like this.

Which meant that Wahlman could go home. He could start living like a normal person again. No more watching his back every second of every day. No more wondering which direction the next bullet was going to come from. He could even try to get back with Kasey.

A sense of elation washed over him. It all seemed too good to be true.

And it was.

Because as he turned to let Dr. Walker know that he needed to go out to his car for a minute, a uniformed soldier walked into the lab.

Army.

Private First Class.

There was a strip of surgical tape on the bridge of his nose and a semi-automatic pistol on his right hip.

His nametag said Bridges.

10

It was the guy Wahlman had questioned out in town last week.

The guy he'd ended up clobbering out on the street on the way back to his car.

PFC Bridges. His face was heavily bruised. He looked angry. Stressed. Like he'd been having a rough time lately. He pulled his pistol out of its holster, walked over to where Wahlman was standing and stared into his eyes.

Dr. Walker took a step toward Bridges. Aggressively, as if she wasn't the least bit concerned about the gun in his hand.

"This is a restricted area," she said. "You're not allowed to be here."

"This man's an imposter," Bridges said. "He's not an admiral. He's not even in the Navy."

"Pardon me?" Dr. Walker said.

"Put the gun away," Wahlman said. "That's an order."

Bridges didn't put the gun away.

"Last week he was pretending to be a senior chief," he

said. "He asked me a bunch of questions. Then he broke my nose when I wanted to see his military ID."

"This is outrageous," Wahlman said. "I've never seen this man before. He's obviously delusional. I would suggest that he be taken into custody and—"

Bridges reached up and ripped the fake mustache off of Wahlman's lip, taking a layer or two of skin along with it.

Dr. Walker's jaw dropped. She backed away from Wahlman and leaned against the glass tank as four more soldiers entered the lab. Two of them stood by with machineguns as Bridges and the other two forced Wahlman to the floor. They patted him down, took his wallet and some loose change and the key to his hotel room. They secured his arms and legs with cuffs and shackles and steel chains and pulled him off of the floor and led him to the elevator. A few minutes later, he was back in the same room he'd been in the first time he'd infiltrated the facility.

"Put him on the table," Bridges said. "No leather restraints this time. Use the cables."

The four guys Bridges seemed to be in charge of led Wahlman to a stainless steel table and forced him onto his back. They tightened the chains that connected the cuffs on his wrists to the shackles on his ankles, and then they looped some plastic-coated steel cables through some of the links and under the table, finally securing everything with a heavy-duty combination lock, the kind you might find on a gate or a toolshed.

"He won't get loose this time," one of the soldiers said.

"Give us the room," Bridges said.

The soldier nodded.

"We'll be out in the hallway if you need us," he said.

The four soldiers exited the room in a single file, the last one closing the door on his way out.

"What are you going to do now?" Wahlman said. "Rough me up? Kill me?"

"General Foss is on his way to the facility," Bridges said. "He should be here sometime this afternoon. You're in big trouble."

"So are you," Wahlman said.

Bridges laughed.

"And just how do you figure that?" he said.

"I'm assuming Major Combs is off today," Wahlman said. "I'm assuming she left you in charge of the security office. Shit rolls downhill, soldier. You know that as well as I do. Someone's going to have to take the blame for the fact that I made it inside again. Someone's going to have to take a fall. You might as well say goodbye to those stripes on your sleeves, because you're not going to have them much longer."

Bridges reached into his pocket and pulled out a set of brass knuckles. He slid his fingers through the holes.

"I was the one who captured you," he said. "If anything, I should get a promotion out of this. At any rate, I feel that it's my obligation to interrogate you to the best of my ability before the general arrives."

"How much do you know about what's going on here?" Wahlman said.

"I'm going to ask the questions, and you're going to answer

them," Bridges said. "That's how this is going to work."

"Just trying to help."

"Help what?"

"Save your career."

"You're full of shit," Bridges said. "Who are you working for?"

"I'm working for me," Wahlman said. "And if you were smart, you'd be working for you, starting right now. Especially if you were telling the truth when I questioned you out in town last week. If you really don't know that much about what's going on here, you might be able to avoid prosecution. General Foss is going to be arrested, along with Dr. Walker and everyone else who's involved with—"

"Shut up," Bridges said. "The only person who's going to be arrested is you. Tell me who you're working for. Now."

"Where are you from?" Wahlman said. "Do you have family back home? Just think about how ashamed they're going to be when they have to tell people what happened to you. Just think about how—"

Bridges stepped forward and punched Wahlman in the ribs with the brass knuckles. It was like being hit with a hammer. Wahlman grunted and coughed and retched, the pain swirling through his core like an electrified tornado.

"That's just a sample," Bridges said. "I have authorization from General Foss to break whatever I need to break. Tell me who you're working for."

"I'm not working for anyone," Wahlman said.

Bridges punched him again, in the exact same spot.

Flashbulbs exploded in front of his eyes. Blue and yellow and red. And then nothing. Total darkness. Like a cave. Cold and black and suffocating. He felt himself sliding deeper and deeper into it, and then he didn't feel anything at all.

11

Twenty-four hours after discussing the idea with her daughter out on the back deck, Kasey was on her way to South Carolina. Her parents had tried to talk her out of it. They'd initially refused to loan her any money for the trip, but had finally given in when she'd started backing out of the driveway with seven dollars in her pocket and half a tank of gas. They'd given her the money she needed and had waved goodbye from the porch as she left, trying but failing miserably to mask the heartache and disappointment and worry they were feeling.

Natalie was the only one who seemed to understand. She'd followed Kasey out to the driveway and had given her a kiss on the cheek and had told her to be careful.

"I love you, Mom," she'd said.

"I love you too, sweetheart. I'll be back in a couple of days."

"Promise?"

"Promise."

Kasey had called Rock's hotel room multiple times before

leaving the house, hoping that he might have gone back there after successfully completing his mission, hoping to hear that all was well and that this whole ordeal would be resolved soon.

Unfortunately, she'd never heard any of that, because he'd never picked up.

She knew he was still a guest there at the hotel, registered under the name Wendell P. Callahan. Which meant that he hadn't left the Myrtle Beach area. Which wasn't necessarily a bad thing. Maybe he was out celebrating. Out having a good time somewhere. Enjoying the sunshine. The ocean breeze. The freedom.

Or maybe he'd been captured and was being held against his will.

Or maybe something even worse than that had happened.

Kasey needed to know.

She'd left the family cell phone with her parents, and had picked up a disposable flip-top at a discount store. Which, as it turned out, had been a good idea. Because, as it turned out, the gas gauge on her car was not working properly, and the half a tank she'd thought she had starting out was really only about a quarter.

The car died less than a hundred miles into the trip. Kasey pulled to the side of the road and called the toll free number on the back of her insurance card and was promptly informed by the guy who answered that her coverage had lapsed and that she would need to go to the company website and renew her policy by credit card if she wanted them to help her.

"I don't have access to a computer right now," she said. "And I don't have a credit card right now either. Just send someone out with a couple of gallons of gasoline and—"

"We don't do that," the guy said.

"You don't do what?"

"Dispatch trucks to random people who call this number."

"I'm not a random person. I'm a client. I just forgot to pay the bill."

"Sorry."

"So you're just going to leave me stranded here on the side of the highway?"

"I can give you the number to the closest service station, if that would help."

He gave her the number, and she called it, and the woman who answered said that it was just her and the tow truck driver working today and that the tow truck driver was out on a run.

"He should be back in an hour or so," the woman said. "You want to wait?"

"I guess I don't have any choice," Kasey said.

"Will you be paying by cash or credit card?"

"Cash."

The woman told Kasey how much it was going to cost to deliver two gallons of gasoline out to the highway on a Sunday afternoon. It was a lot. Kasey thought about trying to negotiate the price, but she figured it would be a waste of time. She agreed to the terms and disconnected and sat there and watched the traffic whiz past and wondered how she was going to get by on the amount of money she had left. She'd planned on getting a hotel room down in Myrtle Beach. That was out now. She'd planned on eating. That was out now too. After paying for the roadside assistance, she would have enough cash to stop at the next exit and fill her gas tank, and that was about it.

She tried Rock's hotel room again. Still no answer.

She considered the possibility of fueling up and then turning around and heading back home to get some more money, but there was a gnawing feeling in her gut that Rock's situation had become urgent and that she needed to get down there as soon as possible.

So she sat there and waited, hoping that it wasn't already too late.

12

Wahlman struggled to regain consciousness. He forced himself awake with a musculoskeletal jerk, the way you do sometimes when you're trying to break out of a nightmare.

Someone had stripped him down to his boxers and had inserted a urinary catheter. The right side of his ribcage throbbed with every breath. Like a rusty old locomotive pulling carloads of agony down a rusty old track from his armpit to his hip. The injury looked as bad as it felt, the yellow and purple bruise extending all the way to the edge of his right nipple.

He looked around. Bridges was gone. There was a lone sentry standing beside the exit, a guy Wahlman had never seen before, a guy with pimples and a long skinny neck and a machinegun.

"What day is it?" Wahlman said, lifting his head up as far as he could, cringing miserably from the effort.

The guard ignored the question. He keyed a walkie-talkie and said, "Unit four to base. The detainee is awake. I repeat, the detainee is awake."

"Copy that," a voice on the other end said.

The guard clipped the walkie-talkie back onto his belt.

"What day is it?" Wahlman said again.

The guard ignored him again. A few minutes later, the doors swung open and two more guards walked in, followed by an officer in full dress uniform.

An officer with two gold stars on each shoulder.

He stepped over to the stainless steel table that Wahlman was cabled to.

"I'm General Foss," he said. "How are you feeling?"

"Terrible," Wahlman said.

"Good. That's the way you should feel. That's the way I want you to feel."

"I'm thirsty. I need water."

"I know who you are," Foss said.

"I know who you are, too," Wahlman said.

"Then you must realize that you're not going to live much longer."

"I realize a lot of things. I realize that you're a piece of shit. I realize that you put hits out on Darrell Renfro and me to ensure that the funding for your little research project would continue to flow."

"The project's not so little," General Foss said. "In fact, it's huge. It's going to be one of mankind's greatest achievements."

"It's some scary-ass shit if you ask me," Wahlman said.

"Nobody asked you. Anyway, I just wanted to let you know that the research will continue, but that we're preparing to destroy this particular facility for reasons that have nothing to do with you or your situation."

"Why should I care about your stupid building?"

"Because you're going to be inside it when it comes down."

"You should let me go," Wahlman said.

"Why should I do that?"

"People are going to be looking for me. The story's going to get out, one way or another. Why add another murder to your list of offenses?"

"Nobody's going to find you," Foss said. "Because there's not going to be anything left to find. Your friends can say whatever they want to say. It's not going to make any difference."

"They know you're producing human clones here."

"How do they know that? Because you told them? There's not going to be any proof that we did anything wrong. There's not going to be any evidence. It's all going to be destroyed. And maybe you didn't hear the news, but human cloning became legal as of last week. So once we move into our new facility, that part of our research won't need to be such a big secret anymore. We can make all the clones we want to make."

"You kill people for money," Wahlman said. "You're nothing but a common criminal."

"Who did I kill?"

"Darrell Renfro, for one. Not you personally, of course. You weren't the one who sunk the knife into his chest. But you arranged for it to happen. And you and your coconspirators will ultimately benefit financially from the fact that it did happen."

"It's true that the formula for the accelerated growth medium is going to make some of us very wealthy men," Foss said. "But it was never about the money for me. It was about securing my place in history. I must admit, I was concerned about the future of the project for a while, mainly because of you, but it looks like everything's going to work out fine now. I would say that my name will be known for many generations to come. Wouldn't you say so?"

"Sure. You'll be right up there with a guy named Frankenstein."

Foss laughed.

"You're a funny man," he said. "And clever too. The admiral's uniform was a nice touch. Would you mind telling me exactly how you acquired it?"

"I borrowed it from a friend," Wahlman said. "I'm going to need to give it back, so I hope you're having it cleaned and pressed."

"Actually, we were able to trace it to its original owner, using the microscopic serial numbers embedded in the buttons. Bet you didn't know about those, huh? Most people don't. Highly classified. Anyway, we know that the uniform belonged to a man named Swanson, and we know that he got into some trouble a few years ago, and we know that his belongings were temporarily placed into the custody of two sailors, a Master-At-Arms named Rock Wahlman and a Master-At-Arms named Joe Balinger. Would Balinger happen to be one of the friends you were talking about? One of the ones who are eventually going to be looking for you?"

Wahlman didn't say anything.

Foss turned and gave the pair of guards who'd escorted him into the room a nod. They exited through the swinging doors and returned a few seconds later with a rolling stainless steel table identical to the one Wahlman was lying on. There was a man on the table. Someone had stripped him down to his underwear and had inserted a urinary catheter. A rectangular sheet of blue surgical paper had been draped over his head. A slit in the paper exposed his nostrils, which were caked with dried blood.

The guards stepped away from the table. General Foss donned a pair of surgical gloves, walked over there and lifted the blue paper from the man's face.

A bolus of rage-infused adrenaline shot through Wahlman's core like a cannonball. The man on the table was Joe Balinger. Both of his ears had bandages on them, and both of the bandages were soaked with blood.

A shiny steel pole had been attached to the table, and a video monitor had been attached to the pole. The monitor showed Joe's heartrate, and his blood pressure, and his oxygen saturation level, all of which were dangerously out of whack. The EKG display resembled the teeth of a sawblade, the spiked waves clipping along at nearly two hundred beats a minute.

"How are you doing?" General Foss said.

"Please," Joe cried. "I can't take it anymore."

Foss shrugged. He walked over to one of the guards, reached down and pulled his pistol out of its holster, walked back to the table and pressed the barrel against Joe's forehead.

The guards retreated warily toward the other side of the room.

Wahlman bucked and thrashed and shouted and pleaded, but it didn't make any difference.

It didn't stop Foss from pulling the trigger.

13

Kasey made it into the Myrtle Beach area at around seven o'clock. She stopped for coffee at a convenience store near the hotel Rock had been staying at and tried calling his room again.

This time, someone answered.

"Hello?" a muffled male voice said.

"Rock?"

There was a long pause, and then a click, and then nothing.

Kasey punched in the number again.

No answer.

She called the front desk to make sure that Wendell P. Callahan hadn't checked out of the hotel. He hadn't. Which meant that Rock had answered the phone and had hung up when he'd heard Kasey's voice. Or that another person was in the room with Rock. Or that another person was in the room alone.

The only scenario that made sense to Kasey at that moment was that someone was in the room with Rock, and it seemed to be a safe bet that whoever it was didn't have Rock's best interest in mind.

Kasey decided to drive over there, knowing that it was probably going to be the most dangerous thing she'd ever done in her life, knowing that it would be smarter to just turn around and drive back home and forget about Rock Wahlman forever.

But knowing that she could never do that, no matter how hard she tried.

Rock had been on her mind the entire time they'd been apart. She longed for him the way she longed for her next breath. She needed him. She loved him. She wanted to be with him for the rest of her life, and she was willing to do whatever it took to make that happen.

On the way to the hotel, she tried to think of something that she might be able to use as a weapon. What she needed was a gun. But she didn't have one. She didn't even have a knife. Or a chain. Or a baseball bat.

She steered into the hotel parking lot and pulled around to the back of the building and found a spot between two pickup trucks. She dug through her purse, found a miniature can of pepper spray her dad had given her a while back and a fingernail file she'd borrowed from her mom. The fingernail file was pointy on the end. Good for extremely close range, but not much else. The pepper spray could be an effective weapon under certain circumstances, but it probably wasn't going to stop anyone who really wanted to get to you, especially in a hotel room, or in the hallway outside a hotel room, or in any other tightly contained area.

So the weapons weren't great, but they were better than nothing.

Kasey switched off the ignition and climbed out of the car. She slid the fingernail file into her back pocket and cupped the pepper spray in her hand and walked around to the front of the building. She stopped and took a couple of deep breaths, entered the lobby through a revolving glass door and made a beeline for the elevator bank, walking purposefully, eyes straight ahead, trying to behave as though she'd been there before and belonged there now.

Rock's room was on the fourth floor. Kasey stepped off the elevator and followed the arrows. She walked past the room nonchalantly, and then she stood in front of a vending machine at the end of the hallway and pretended to be deliberating over which snack to buy. She stood there for a long time. Nothing happened for a long time. Then the elevator dinged and a young lady pushed a stainless steel cart out into the corridor. There was a domed plate on the cart and some silverware rolled up into a cloth napkin and an unopened bottle of beer. The young lady walked to the room directly across the hall from Rock's room and knocked on the door. Waited. Knocked again. Waited some more. Knocked some more.

"Hey," Kasey said, stepping away from the vending machine and walking toward the young lady.

"Did you order a steak and a salad?" the young lady said.

"Yes. Thank you."

"Want me to open the beer for you?"

"No thanks. I have an opener in my room."

Kasey reached into her pocket and pulled out the last of her money and handed it to the young lady for a tip.

"Thanks," the young lady said. "Have a nice evening."

"You too," Kasey said.

The young lady walked back to the elevator bank. Pushed the button. Stepped into the carriage.

Kasey waited until the elevator doors closed completely, and then she unrolled the napkin and grabbed the steak knife and slid it into her back pocket, next to the fingernail file. She wheeled the cart across the hall and knocked on the door to Rock's room. The peephole darkened and the chain rattled and the door swung open slowly. A guy wearing an extremely wrinkled United States Navy uniform and smelling strongly of whiskey and tobacco stood there and stared down at the cart.

"What's that?" he said.

Kasey shot him in the face with pepper spray. As he staggered backward and tripped over his own feet and fell to the floor, Kasey rammed the cart forward and pushed her way into the room and slammed the door shut.

"Room service," she said, straddling the drunken sailor's fat belly and pressing the blade of the steak knife against his right jugular.

"Wait," the guy said. "I'm just—"

"Where is he?" Kasey said.

"Who?"

Kasey pressed down harder with the blade. A scabbed-over nick, probably from the last time the guy shaved, opened up and started bleeding, the bright red trail trickling down the guy's double chin and blooming like a miniature carnation on the inside of his collar.

"Where is he?" Kasey said again.

"You talking about Callahan?"

"Yes."

"He told me to go ahead and leave if he wasn't back in two hours," the guy said. "I didn't think it would do any harm to stay here in the room for a night or two."

"Wait," Kasey said. "Start over. I want to know exactly what happened."

The guy told Kasey exactly what had happened. He told her about the tall guy named Callahan who had approached him in line at the employment agency, about accepting the job offer, about the barbershop and the uniforms and getting through the gate at the research facility, about waiting in the parking lot for two hours and then an extra ten minutes just in case, about driving back to the hotel and taking the elevator up to the room to retrieve the monetary compensation that Callahan had left there for him.

"I figured the room was paid for already," he said. "No point in letting it go to waste."

"What's your name?" Kasey said.

"Puhler. Can you let me up now? I think I'm bleeding."

"I'm going to need your help finding Callahan."

"That's no problem," Puhler said. "The building he went into is called The Box. And that's what it looks like. A big concrete box. No windows, no doors. You have to use some kind of pneumatic transport system to get inside. I can tell you where the building is, but I'm not going back there, if that's what you had in mind."

"That's exactly what I had mind," Kasey said.

"Not going to happen."

"Is going to happen."

"You can't make me do something I don't want to do," Puhler said. "Anyway, Callahan must have gotten caught impersonating an officer. They're not going to let anyone through that gate now, not without a thorough identification check. And Callahan might not even be there anymore. They might have taken him somewhere else."

"I don't think they took him anywhere else," Kasey said. "If you're detaining someone, any sort of movement increases the risk of escape—which is something that Callahan is really good at, and something his captors know he's really good at. If Callahan's still alive, I'm pretty sure he's still in that building."

"What do you mean if he's still alive?"

"Long story."

"I don't think I want to know."

"I don't think you do either. Tell me how to get to the research facility."

Puhler gazed up at the ceiling. His eyes looked like he'd been rubbing them with pencil erasers. He told Kasey how to get to the research facility from the hotel.

"But it doesn't really matter if he's still in that building or not," he said. "Security's going to be tight as a toenail now."

"Tight as a toenail?"

"Or something. I need coffee."

Kasey eased the blade away from Puhler's throat. She could tell that he was pretty drunk. There was an empty whiskey bottle on the nightstand, and she doubted that he'd shared any with anyone.

"I'll get you some coffee," she said. "Then we're going to try to figure this out."

14

General Foss pushed his way through the swinging doors without saying another word. One of the guards who'd escorted him into the room followed him out to the hallway. The other one put some gloves on and walked over and switched off the video monitor and wiped the blood and bone fragments off the shiny steel pole with a paper towel. He covered Joe's lifeless body with a sheet and wheeled him out of the room, showing no more emotion that he might have shown pushing a wheelbarrow full of bricks. The guard who'd been there when Wahlman woke up went back to his spot beside the door.

Wahlman's ears were still ringing from the pistol report, and his heart was still trying to pound its way out of his chest, and the Pain Train was still roaring down the track, whistling and smoking and rattling its way through flesh and bone and internal organs. Wahlman wondered if the brass knuckles had been traded for a jackhammer at some point. The intensity of the pain just kept getting worse, and there was nothing he could do about it. He couldn't even reposition himself.

He stared up at the ceiling, felt a tear escape from the corner of his right eye. Joe Balinger had been a friend for many years. An all-around good guy. One of the best. Wahlman remembered that he'd been planning to get married, but he couldn't remember his fiancé's name. Maybe he'd never mentioned it. He would have been a good husband and a good dad.

Wahlman looked down at the urine that was pooled at the curve of the catheter tubing. It was dark amber in color, a sign of dehydration. Maybe they were going to make him lie there and die of thirst.

"I need water," he said.

The guard stared straight ahead. He didn't say anything.

Wahlman had no idea what time it was, or even what day it was. There were no clocks in the room, no windows. He looked over at the line of supply cabinets against the wall. The glass he'd shattered on his previous visit to the facility had been replaced. Everything looked as good as new. And now, according to General Foss, it was all going to be destroyed. Maybe Foss had been lying about that. Why would they have gone to all the trouble of repairing the supply cabinet just so they could blow it up? Didn't make sense.

Wahlman kept thinking about it until he couldn't think anymore. He closed his eyes and drifted into a dream-saturated semiconscious state that teetered on the precipice of true sleep, his brain probably sensing that going all the way would mean never coming back. In his dream, or his hallucination, or whatever it was, he was in Florida, and

Kasey Stielson was his wife, and he'd finally gotten his private investigator's license, and he was in an office, sitting behind a desk, talking to a potential client, a very beautiful woman with dark hair and eyes as warm as cinnamon toast.

Wahlman shuffled through some papers.

"What was your name again?" he said.

"Why do you need to know that?" the woman said.

"It's just one of my standard questions. We can come back to it. So tell me, what brings you to my office today?"

"He's dead, isn't he?"

"Ma'am?"

"The man I was going to marry. The man who was going to be the father of my children. He's dead, and it's your fault."

The woman opened her purse and pulled out a knife and stabbed Wahlman in the arm with it.

"Don't do that," Wahlman said.

He opened his eyes. A man wearing a white lab coat and a surgical mask was standing beside the table tapping air bubbles out of a syringe.

"I put an IV needle in your left arm," the man said. "I'm going to give you something for pain, and then I'm going to start some fluids."

"Why?" Wahlman said.

"To keep you hydrated."

"Why?"

"Because General Foss told me to."

"General Foss made it clear that I don't have long to live," Wahlman said. "So why is he trying to keep me alive?"

"You'll have to ask him about that."

The man injected the contents of the syringe into the tubing taped to Wahlman's left arm.

The effects were immediate.

As if someone had swept the pain away with a brush.

Wahlman felt like a million bucks. He might have done a cartwheel if he hadn't been tied down with steel cables.

The man spiked a liter of normal saline and bled the air out of a tubing set and adjusted the drip with a thumb clamp.

"Thank you," Wahlman said. "I feel much better now. I think I'll just go on home."

The man laughed. He gathered his things and threw away the plastic wrappers from the IV supplies and exited the room.

A few minutes later, PFC Bridges walked in.

"The pain medicine was the general's idea," Bridges said.

"Tell him I said thanks."

"I was against it."

"I'm not surprised," Wahlman said.

"The IV drip was my idea."

"Okay."

"We're going to keep you going until the demolition crew gets here tomorrow morning. Should be quite a show."

"If you consider cold-blooded murder to be a show," Wahlman said.

Bridges shrugged.

"The general has arranged for me to be his personal assistant," he said, proudly. "We're going to be looking at a live video feed. I might even make some popcorn to eat while I watch."

Wahlman wanted to grab Bridges by the shirt and make him eat his own front teeth.

"What about the rest of the staff?" he said.

"They've all been notified that we're bugging out. Almost everyone who was here for the weekend is gone. Now, if you'll shut up for a minute or two, I need to go ahead and explain exactly how everything's going to go down tomorrow."

"Why would you want to do that?" Wahlman said.

"Because the general told me to. And because I want to see the expression on your face when you find out how horrible the last few hours of your life are going to be."

"The expression on my face isn't going to change," Wahlman said. "Not for a piece of shit like you."

Bridges reached into his pocket and pulled out the brass knuckles.

"We'll see about that," he said.

15

Kasey called room service and ordered a pot of coffee. When it came, she politely asked Puhler to answer the door, hoping to avoid a second encounter with the young lady she'd talked to in the hallway earlier. Because of the fraudulent procurement of the stainless steel cart with the domed plate and the silverware rolled up into a cloth napkin and the unopened bottle of beer on it. As it turned out, a young man delivered the coffee. Puhler tipped him and sent him on his way.

Kasey sat across from Puhler at the little round wooden table in the corner and they shared the steak and the salad and an overcooked baked potato and some butter and a roll. Puhler kept eyeing the bottle of beer. Kasey kept shoving more coffee in front of him.

"I need you to sober up," she said. "So we can figure this out."

"You keep saying *we*," Puhler said. "I told you I'm not going back there."

"Yes you are."

"No I'm not."

"I need your help."

"Sorry," Puhler said. "But I almost had a heart attack the first time. Now you're telling me that there are killers behind those walls? That kind of shit's not for me. I'm going to hitch a ride back to the ferry, and I'm going to buy a ticket to cross the bay, and I'm going to be standing back in line at the employment agency tomorrow morning."

"How much did Callahan pay you?" Kasey said.

"I don't think that's any of your business."

"Tell me how much he paid you. I'll double it. All you have to do is—"

"You don't have any money," Puhler said. "You didn't even have enough to tip the guy for the coffee."

"My father's very wealthy," Kasey said. "I'll have the money wired here as soon as we're finished. How much did Callahan pay you?"

"Five hundred."

Kasey figured he was lying. She didn't care.

"I'll give you a thousand," she said.

Puhler picked a piece of meat from between his teeth with a fingernail.

He sipped his coffee.

"How can I be sure you're going to pay me?" he said.

"You can hold the keys to my car until we're finished. How about that?"

Puhler shrugged.

"I'll think about it," he said.

"Or how about this," Kasey said. "I'll call the shore patrol over in Myrtle Beach and tell them that an inebriated man wearing a United States Navy uniform with Master-At-Arms insignias on the rank patches is giving me a hard time. They'll take one look at you and arrest you on the spot, and when they find out that you're wearing the United States Navy uniform illegally, they'll—"

"All right," Puhler said. "A thousand bucks."

"Great. So let's talk about how we're going to get inside."

"I don't think it's really going to be much of a problem," Puhler said.

"Why do you say that?"

"I overheard some things while I was sitting out in the parking lot. Apparently they're going to be moving to a different location. Everyone's going to be gone by five o'clock in the morning. Everyone but Callahan."

"Why didn't you tell me that before?"

"Must have slipped my mind."

"Maybe because you sat here and drank a fifth of bourbon all by yourself."

"Maybe."

"Or maybe because you just didn't feel compelled to help me until I threatened to call the shore patrol."

"Maybe."

Kasey was starting to wonder if she could trust anything that was coming from Puhler's mouth, including the business about the operation moving to a different location.

"Why everyone but Callahan?" she said. "Why are they leaving him there by himself?"

"I don't know. I didn't catch that part. And they didn't

refer to Callahan by his name. They called him *the general's detainee.* I just figured that's who they were talking about. This was right before I started the car and drove away. If I'd stayed much longer, I probably would have been a detainee too."

"Probably. I want to get to the facility as soon as possible. Let's go ahead and—"

"The ferries don't start running until four-thirty," Puhler said. "So there's no point in thinking about doing anything before then. We can get some sleep, head out around four."

Kasey glanced over at the bed.

"I hope you don't think you're staying in this room tonight," she said.

"Where else am I supposed to stay?"

"You can sleep in the rental car."

"But I was here first," Puhler said.

"You're a squatter. You don't belong here."

"But—"

"Plus, I'm going to be paying you a lot of money. I get the room. You get the car. End of discussion."

Puhler grabbed the bottle of beer, rested the edge of the cap against the edge of the table, popped it off by slamming it with the butt of his hand.

"Fine," he said. "But don't complain about the way I smell after sweating my ass off out there in the car all night."

"Don't worry," Kasey said. "I'll wake you up in plenty of time to take a shower."

16

The pain medicine Wahlman had received was no match for the fresh set of bruises.

No match at all.

PFC Bridges had worked on the left side of his ribcage this time.

Now there were two locomotives, one on each side of Wahlman's body, two enormous greasy black engines cranking it out down two wobbly sets of tracks, almost like a competition, like some sort of sadistic race where the grand prize was a bucketful of misery.

Choo! Choo!

Right now the left side was winning, but the right side was starting to pick up speed again. Wahlman figured the two would be neck and neck in a little while. He clenched his teeth and flexed his muscles and grunted and shouted and writhed.

Before leaving the room, Bridges had explained how everything was supposed to go down tomorrow morning.

At 03:00, a pair of guards would come and wheel the

table Wahlman was lying on into a different room, a room closer to the center of the basement. At 03:30, the demolition experts would arrive and place a number of explosive charges at a number of load-bearing locations within the facility. A computerized timer would relay an electrical pulse to the charges at a prescribed time, resulting is a series of explosions that would cause the building to collapse in on itself.

And that would be that.

Wahlman was going to spend the next few hours in agonizing pain, and then he was going to die. Those were the facts, and there was nothing he could do to change them. He was too weak to put up any sort of fight, even if an opportunity presented itself. The cuffs and shackles and chains and cables were extreme overkill now. He wasn't sure that he could even stand up on his own at this point.

It had been a pretty good life, for the most part. The orphanage had been kind of tough sometimes, but at least they'd provided him with the basic necessities. He'd thrived as a law enforcement officer in the Navy, and there were times he wished he'd stayed in for another ten years. He'd laughed a lot and loved a lot and had been to places most people only dreamt about. It had been a pretty good life, but now it was over. And he was okay with that. He wasn't afraid to die. He only hoped that the gross injustices he and Darrell Renfro had been dealt would eventually come to light, and that all of the dealers would eventually get what they deserved.

He took some quick and shallow breaths, opened his eyes

and looked around. The guy with the machinegun was still standing at the door. Still staring straight ahead.

"Please," Wahlman said. "I need water. Just a sip."

"I'm not supposed to talk to you," the guard said.

His voice was deep and raspy. Like he'd recently swallowed a handful of sand or something.

"I'm dying," Wahlman said. "What harm could it possibly do to give me a drink of water?"

The guard leaned his gun against the fat strip of steel molding that surrounded the door frame, crossed the room and grabbed a little paper cup from a little plastic dispenser that was mounted to the wall over the sink. He filled the cup with tap water, walked over to the table and held it to Wahlman's lips.

The guard was a corporal. His nametag said McGaff.

"I could get in big trouble for doing this," he said.

Wahlman slurped the water into his mouth, absorbing it like a sponge.

"Thank you," he said.

"Let me know if you want some more. I'm here for the duration."

"What time is it now?"

"Almost midnight."

"Saturday?"

"Sunday," Corporal McGaff said.

He tossed the paper cup into the trashcan, walked back to the door and picked up his gun and stood there and stared straight ahead.

17

Kasey stared at the digital clock on the nightstand until the alarm went off. She climbed out of bed, took a quick shower, walked out to the parking lot.

Rock's rental car was gone.

Which meant that Puhler was gone.

Which meant that he was a total piece of shit. A total waste of oxygen.

Maybe he'd made another trip to the liquor store. Maybe he was sleeping it off on a park bench somewhere. Kasey felt stupid for trusting him to do what he said he was going to do, stupid for not taking the keys to the rental car and hiding them somewhere. She started walking toward her car to see how much gas she had left, and then she remembered that her gauge wasn't working.

Shit.

She hadn't thought to check the odometer when she filled up, but she knew she'd driven at least a couple of hundred miles since then. Maybe she still had around half a tank.

It seemed absurd that Rock's life might depend on such a trivial matter, but apparently that was the case. If there had been more time, Kasey would have called her dad and asked for more money, just to be on the safe side. But it was almost four already, and Rock was going to be left alone at the facility at five, and there was no telling what would happen after that. Nothing good, that was for sure.

So Kasey needed to get moving. Not in an hour or so, the time it would take to make the call to her dad and fill out the forms and wait at the front desk for the transfer approval codes. She needed to get moving now. She would steal some gasoline if she had to. She would do whatever it took to get to Rock in time and get him out of the facility safely.

She walked to her car, climbed in and started the engine, steered out of the hotel parking lot and headed toward the dock to catch the ferry.

The ferry.

Shit.

That was going to cost money too. Money that Kasey didn't have.

She made a U-turn. She was going to have to go back to the hotel and call her dad and wait for a money transfer to go through. No choice.

She pounded on the dashboard with her fist. She felt as frustrated as she'd ever felt in her life. She stopped at an intersection, thought about running the red light, but didn't. The way things had been going, she would probably end up getting pulled over, which would waste even more time.

While she was sitting there waiting for the light to change, she pressed the button to spray some fluid onto the windshield, hoping to wash away some of the grime and insect carcasses from the interstate. The wiper on the driver side scooted noisily about halfway into its arc, and then it stopped completely. Kasey ducked down and squinted and saw that a folded piece of paper had been stuffed under the blade. She switched off the wipers and rolled the window down and reached out and grabbed the paper and unfolded it.

Five twenty dollar bills fell in her lap.

She used the miniature flashlight that she kept on her keychain to read the note.

> *Dear Kasey,*
>
> *Sorry about leaving, but I just couldn't go through with it. I hope you're able to do what you set out to do. I hope this helps.*
>
> *Puhler*

So maybe he wasn't a total waste of oxygen after all.

Kasey didn't really blame Puhler for bailing on her. He'd obviously decided that returning to the research facility was just too much of a risk, no matter how much money was involved. And he was right. A thousand dollars wasn't enough. A million wouldn't have been enough. Not for the potential danger he would have been facing. Not if his heart wasn't in it.

Kasey's heart was in it.

And a hundred dollars would definitely help.

A hundred dollars would make all the difference.

Kasey wadded the note into a ball and tossed it over onto the passenger side floorboard and waited for the light to turn green. As soon as it did, she made another U-turn and headed back toward the dock, determined more than ever to make it across the bay to the research facility by five, determined more than ever to do whatever needed to be done once she got there.

18

Most of the power to the facility had been shut down hours ago.

PFC Bridges was sitting in the security office with General Foss and Corporal McGaff, drinking coffee and watching live video feeds from the handful of cameras that were still in operation. Foss had made it clear that the three of them would be the last people to leave the facility—other than Wahlman, of course, who wasn't ever going to leave.

Bridges didn't care much for the arrangement, although he was quite aware of the tradition behind the general's decision to set it up that way.

The phone on the desk rang.

"That's going to be Kelsoe again," Foss said, staring into one of the monitors. "Looks like they're about finished."

Kelsoe was the foreman on the demolition crew. He'd been checking in every thirty minutes or so.

Bridges switched the call to speakerphone and picked up the receiver.

"Security," he said.

"It's me again," Kelsoe said. "We're about to wrap things up. Just need to activate the timer. You want it set for one hour, right?"

Bridges looked at Foss.

Foss nodded.

"Affirmative," Bridges said. "One hour."

There was a brief period of silence, followed by a series of electronic beeps.

"Okay," Kelsoe said. "The clock is ticking."

"General Foss wants you guys to use the ladders and the service walkways to get back outside," Bridges said.

"Right. We already talked about that."

"Just wanted to make sure you understood."

"Yeah. And it's kind of a long walk, so I better get going. Have a great day."

Kelsoe disconnected.

Bridges lowered the receiver back into its cradle.

"Sir, I think we should head on up to the PTS now," he said.

"We're going to wait until the demo crew makes it outside," General Foss said. "Then we're going to wait until they climb into their truck and drive away. Shouldn't take long. Ten minutes max. That'll leave us plenty of time to take the PTS up to the front portal."

"There are three of us, sir. Which means that—"

"Relax," Foss said. "We'll have plenty of time."

Bridges tried to relax, but he couldn't. He stared at the video monitors, hoping that he didn't look as anxious as he felt. It was quite an honor to be selected as the general's personal assistant, and he didn't want to get off to a bad start by questioning the general's judgement on this matter.

But he also didn't want to get blown to bits.

The demolition crew consisted of four men. Bridges watched as they made their way into the tunnels and up the ladders and finally through the heavy steel service hatch, emerging into the harsh glare of the exterior lights about fifty feet west of the front guard shack. They walked over to the gate and loaded their tools into the back of their van, which was parked beside the dark green luxury sedan that Bridges would eventually be using to transport General Foss and Corporal McGaff away from the facility.

"Grab some flashlights," Foss said.

He stood and walked over to the electrical panel and started switching off generators, killing power to everything except the elevators and the pneumatic transport system. The overhead lights in the security office went dark, as did the video monitors.

Bridges passed a flashlight to Corporal McGaff, and then he handed one to the general.

"Here you go, sir," he said. "We really should be going now."

"That's why I shut everything down," Foss said, gruffly. "Because we are going now."

"Yes, sir."

Bridges looked at his watch. In forty-seven minutes, the building would be reduced to rubble. Forty-seven minutes was plenty of time for the three of them to make it outside and drive far enough away to escape any effects from the blast. It was at least twice as much time as they actually needed. Bridges knew that. But he also knew that shit happened. If he had been running the show, he would have set the timer for two hours. Maybe even three.

He opened the door and exited the security office. General Foss was a couple of steps behind him, and Corporal McGaff was a couple of steps behind General Foss. They made it to the elevator and up one floor, and then they walked through the corridor that led to the PTS portal. Bridges set the pace, which was somewhere between a brisk walk and a trot. When they made it to within a few feet of the portal, General Foss stopped and turned and rested his hand on Corporal McGaff's shoulder.

"Private Bridges and I will go first," Foss said. "You'll see the green light for the capsule-return mode soon after we make it out to the shack."

"Yes, sir," McGaff said.

Bridges helped the general into the passenger seat, and a minute or so later they were whizzing through the system like an enormous bullet that had been shot from the barrel of an enormous rifle. They would make it to the shack in less than a minute. Then, two or three minutes after that, McGaff would join them and they would all climb into the dark green sedan and wave goodbye to The Box and everything inside it, including the man tied to the table in the basement.

Bridges felt kind of silly now for worrying so much. He smiled, knowing what a great assignment this was going to be, knowing that a series of quick promotions would be coming his way, figuring he would be wearing sergeant's stripes in less than two years. Everything was going to be great from this point forward. Everything was going to work out just fine.

"What's that noise?" General Foss said. "And why are we slowing down?"

Bridges didn't know what that noise was.

And he didn't know why they were slowing down.

"I don't know, sir," he said.

A few seconds later, they weren't slowing down anymore.

A few seconds later, they had come to a complete stop.

"What's going on?" Foss said.

Bridges frantically started pushing buttons and flipping switches, but nothing he did made any difference. The PTS capsule wouldn't move forward, toward the portal in the front guard shack, and it wouldn't move backward, toward the portal they'd just come from. It wouldn't move an inch in either direction.

"I think we're stuck, sir," Bridges said.

"What do you mean we're stuck? We can't be stuck. Get us out of here, private. That's an order."

"I'm trying, sir."

"Just open the door. We'll climb out and crawl the rest of the way."

"The door won't open, sir. It's designed to stay closed while the capsule is inside the transit tube."

"Isn't there some sort of emergency escape hatch?"

"No, sir."

"Why not?"

"It's a safety issue, sir. Regarding the extreme difference in pressure on the other side of the capsule."

Foss started pounding on the instrument console in front of him.

"What do people usually do when one of these things gets stuck?" he said.

"I've never heard of anything like this happening before," Bridges said. "But the manual they gave us when we were in training for these systems said that any sort of malfunction should be reported to the maintenance department immediately."

"The maintenance department left hours ago."

"Yes, sir."

"So what are we going to do?"

"I don't know, sir."

"McGaff. He's waiting for the capsule to come back to him. When it doesn't, he's going to know something is wrong. Would it be possible for him to shut the power off and crawl down here and push us through manually?"

Bridges thought about that.

"Yes, sir," he said. "I think that would work."

"How much time do we have?"

"Forty-one minutes, sir."

A dry growl came from somewhere deep in the back of the general's throat.

"That's not going to be enough, is it?" he said.

"No, sir," Bridges said. "I don't think it is."

19

"My name is Rock Wahlman. In exactly thirty-seven minutes and twenty-nine seconds, I'm going to die."

Before the guards had come to transport Wahlman to the room he was in now, the man wearing the white lab coat and the surgical mask had returned and had administered another dose of IV pain medicine, along with some sort of stimulant, a drug that had instantly jolted Wahlman into a state of extreme hyperawareness. Currently pain-free and super-duper energized, he felt like climbing off the table and running a marathon or two just for fun.

Of course he couldn't really climb off the table. He couldn't do anything except watch the screen on the laptop computer that had been placed in front of him. Which, as of several minutes ago, had become the only source of light in the room.

37:28...

37:27...

37.26...

"Rock," a distant female voice shouted. "Rock, are you here?"

Wahlman ignored the voice, which was obviously an auditory hallucination, the result of sleep deprivation and the intravenous chemical cocktail he'd received. He figured the medication had been ordered to ensure that he would be awake and alert right up to the last minute, right up to the point where the explosive charges went off and the building started crumbing down on top of him.

He continued talking out loud, telling his story, hoping that the security cameras were picking it up, hoping that someone would eventually hear what he was saying.

The female voice interrupted him again, calling out his name again.

The voice seemed closer this time.

It seemed to be getting closer by the second.

The door to the room creaked open. Wahlman tilted his head to the left and saw a pinpoint of light, a bright little blueish-white star that was slowly moving toward him.

"Go away," he said. "You're not real."

"Rock? It's me. Kasey."

A split second before he repeated the command for the hallucination to go away, Wahlman felt a soft cool hand grip his left forearm.

"Kasey?" he said.

"What have they done to you?"

"Kasey? Is that really you? How did you find this place? How did you—"

"I'll tell you all about it later. Right now I just want to get you out of here."

"No. You need to run as fast as you can. See the numbers

counting down on that monitor over there? When those numbers get to zero, some electronic relays are going to trigger some explosive charges and this whole building is going to come down like a sandcastle at high tide. You need to get out of here. Now."

"I'm not leaving without you," Kasey said.

"They tied me to the table with steel cables. The cables are secured with a padlock. There's just not enough time."

"I walked into some sort of maintenance room a few minutes ago. There were tools in there. Just tell me what I need."

"You need to go. You need to get as far away from here as possible."

"I'm not leaving without you," Kasey said again.

"Then you're going to die."

"Okay."

Wahlman felt like shouting, but he didn't. Because he knew it wouldn't do any good. Because he knew Kasey. Once she had her mind set on doing something, there was no talking her out of it.

"Why do you have to be so stubborn?" he said.

"Just tell me what kind of tool I need."

"Bolt cutters," Wahlman said. "Or a hacksaw. Or even a hatchet, if that's all you can find. Bolt cutters would be best."

"What do bolt cutters look like?"

"They have long handles. Maybe two feet long. Blades on the end that mate up flush with each other."

"I'll be right back," Kasey said.

She returned a couple of minutes later with a set of bolt

cutters and a hacksaw and a hatchet and a battery-powered lantern.

"Just snip the lock with the bolt cutters," Wahlman said.

Kasey snipped the lock with the bolt cutters. She unwound the steel cables, and then she cut the chains on the handcuffs and shackles.

Wahlman sat up, fought off a wave of vertigo, climbed off of the table and held Kasey in his arms and kissed her and told her how much he loved her.

"I love you too," she said. "Think we should be going now?"

"I think that would be a good idea."

"We need to find you some clothes. Or at least some shoes."

"There's no time for that. I'll be all right."

Kasey picked up the lantern.

"Follow me," she said.

Wahlman used the bolt cutters to free himself from the drainage bag that was attached to his catheter, and then he grabbed the hatchet and followed Kasey out of the room.

"How are we going to get out of the building?" Wahlman said. "The pneumatic transport system requires a fingerprint scan and an access code. And even if we were able to get past all that, someone cut the power a while ago. The system isn't even going to be—"

"Actually, the system is still up and running," Kasey said. "But we're not going to be using it. We're going to get out the same way I got in."

She led Wahlman through a disorienting series of

hallways and into an alcove that housed what appeared to be the central vacuum unit for the PTS. She turned the knob on an unmarked red door and exited into a walkway with a steel grate for a floor and a concrete ceiling that was only about six feet high. Wahlman had to stoop as he entered the space, and the grate was rough on his bare feet, and urine from the severed catheter was trickling down his right leg, but none of that mattered, none of it prevented him from breaking into a trot to keep up with Kasey as she hustled toward a steel ladder at the far end of the tunnel.

A situation that had seemed utterly hopeless only minutes ago now promised to be one of the best days of Rock Wahlman's life. He gripped the hatchet and used it as an extension of his right hand as he mounted the ladder, taking it one slippery rung at a time, guided by the light from Kasey's lantern, which was spilling over the edge of the platform above.

Wahlman was almost to the top, only a second or two from joining Kasey on the next level, when a deep and raspy male voice shouted, "Stop, or I'll shoot!"

20

Wahlman recognized the voice.

It was Corporal McGaff, the guard who'd been posted by the door in the medical supply room, the guard who'd stood there for hours, at least a double shift, maybe a triple.

Wahlman wondered why he was still in the building.

But he didn't wonder for long.

Because it didn't really matter.

The guard was in the way, which meant that the guard would have to be taken out of the way.

Amped on adrenaline and the super-therapeutic dose of drugs he'd been given, Wahlman climbed onto the platform and positioned himself between Kasey and Corporal McGaff, who was still holding the machinegun he'd been holding earlier.

McGaff aimed the barrel of the gun directly at Wahlman's core.

"Drop it," Wahlman said.

"I don't want to shoot you, man."

"I know you don't. So drop the rifle. We'll walk out of

here together. You can go your way, and I'll go mine."

Sweat beaded on McGaff's forehead. He was thinking it over. Considering his options.

He was obviously very nervous, unsteady, the tip of the gun barrel jittering like the needle on a pressure gauge, a needle that had crept into the red zone, a needle that was extremely close to being pegged.

He tightened his grip on the handguard, clicked off the safety.

"What happened to General Foss and Private Bridges?" he said.

"I don't know," Wahlman said.

"I'm going to have to take you into custody."

"No you're not."

"I can't just let you go."

"Sure you can."

Something clattered metallically against the wall to McGaff's left. Something with some weight. Probably a coin from one of Kasey's pockets. Probably a penny or a nickel or a dime or a quarter, discreetly tossed to the side of the walkway to create a momentary diversion. McGaff instinctively made a slight turn toward the disturbance, and the barrel of the gun made a slight turn with him, and with absolutely no hesitation, Wahlman reared back and threw the hatchet as hard as he could, the way he would have thrown a fastball in the bottom of the ninth with bases loaded and two outs and a full count on the guy at the plate. The steel head and the hardwood handle whizzed through the air end-over-end, came to an abrupt stop when the razor-sharp blade thudded deeply into the center of McGaff's chest. An earsplitting burst of machinegun fire echoed through the space as he collapsed forward onto the grate, the weight of his body pushing the heavy cutting tool even deeper into his sternum.

Wahlman took a few steps forward, leaned down and grabbed the automatic rifle.

"I didn't want to kill him," he said.

"You didn't have a choice," Kasey said.

"He was all right. He gave me water."

"He should have let you go. He chose not to."

Wahlman nodded.

"Foss and Bridges," he said. "Any idea what he was talking about?"

"Who are Foss and Bridges?"

"Foss is a two-star general. He's in charge of the entire operation. Bridges is his personal assistant."

"I have a feeling they might be stuck somewhere in the PTS," Kasey said.

"Because of something you did?" Wahlman said.

"Yes."

"This day just keeps getting better and better."

"We should go."

"Lead the way," Wahlman said. "I'll be right behind you."

21

After a two-hour visit to an urgent care center and a forty-eight hour visit to the bed in his hotel room, Wahlman had delivered a ten-page written statement and the disc-shaped audio recording device to one of the investigative reporters he'd spoken to previously. The story broke a day and a half later. A day and a half after that, Wahlman joined Kasey for a late breakfast at the little mom-and-pop diner across the street from the hotel. A waitress named Justine brought coffee and asked if they were ready to order.

"We still need a few minutes," Wahlman said.

"That's fine," Justine said. "I'll check back in a little while."

She stepped away and refilled the cups at the next booth.

Wahlman wore jeans and a t-shirt and a nice pair of leather work boots, all purchased by Kasey with money her parents had wired from somewhere in Virginia. None of Wahlman's ribs were broken, but they were still very sore. His chest looked like someone had spilled several different colors of ink on it.

"Dad said we can stay at the lake house in Tennessee," Kasey said, tearing a packet of sugar open and stirring it into her coffee. "He said we can stay there as long as we want to."

"I'll have to take care of the situation down in New Orleans first," Wahlman said. "It shouldn't take long, now that the word is out about what was going on. They'll have to book me, but I should be able to get out on bail."

"At least nobody is trying to kill you now."

"Yeah. So I can breathe a little easier."

"A lot easier."

"I couldn't have done it without you."

"I know."

"You're the best thing that ever happened to me."

"I know."

Kasey had provided some of the details behind her experience at the research facility while Wahlman was convalescing in the hotel room. She'd left her car on the side of the highway and had crawled through the tunnel of foliage and had seen that the front gate was wide open and that two vehicles had been parked there—an unmarked cargo van, which meant nothing to Kasey, and a dark green luxury sedan with a small United States Army flag attached to the antenna and a front plate with two big stars on it, which meant plenty. She'd watched from the edge of the woods as four men wearing dirty white coveralls emerged from a metal hatch that was flush with the ground. The men threw some tools into the back of the van and climbed in, and a few seconds later the headlights came on and the van sped away. Figuring that a general and his or her entourage wouldn't be using a grimy service tunnel to get to the green luxury sedan—the only other vehicle in sight—Kasey ran to the guard shack and walked inside and saw the portal to the pneumatic transport system. There was a narrow cot in one corner of the shack with a thin mattress on it. Kasey rolled the mattress up and tied it with a sheet and dropped it into the dark and empty space behind the slot for the PTS capsule and watched it disappear into the blackness. She had no idea what kind of effect the fat cushiony foreign object would have on the system, but she hoped that it would slow the general and his crew down long enough for her to make it over to the service hatch. Of course it had ultimately done a lot more than that. It had caused General Foss and PFC Bridges to be trapped inside the system, somewhere along the transit tube, where they'd remained until the percussive wave from the explosive charges swept by, causing their lungs to slowly and painfully fill with blood.

A horrible way to die, but then they were pretty horrible guys. The only one Wahlman felt bad about was McGaff. He wished it could have gone differently with him.

He thought about it as he sat there in the little mom-and-pop diner and sipped his coffee, and he thought about everything that Kasey had done for him. Everything in the last few days, and everything since the day he'd met her.

"You're amazing," he said.

"I know," she said.

"Will you marry me?"

"I'll think about it."

Kasey smiled.

Wahlman smiled back.

He leaned forward and she leaned forward and they met in the middle and kissed, and they talked some more and drank another cup of coffee and decided to skip breakfast and go on back to the hotel for a while.

Thanks so much for reading END GAME!

For occasional updates and special offers, please visit my website and sign up for my newsletter.

My Nicholas Colt thriller series includes these full-length novels: AMERICAN P.I., LADY 52, POCKET-47, CROSSCUT, SNUFF TAG 9, KEY DEATH, BLOOD TATTOO, SYCAMORE BLUFF, and THE REACHER FILES: FUGITIVE.

THE REACHER FILES: VELOCITY takes the series in a new direction, and sets the stage for THE BLOOD NOTEBOOKS.

And now, for the first time, 4 NICHOLAS COLT NOVELS have been published together in a box set at a special low price.

All of my books are lendable, so feel free to share them with a friend at no additional cost.

All reviews are much appreciated!

Thanks again, and happy reading!

Jude